PETAL AND POPPY

AND THE

MYSTERY VALENTINE

LISA CLOUGH

AND

ED BRIANT

Green Light Readers

HOUGHTON MIFFLIN HARCOURT

Boston New York

For information about permission to reproduce selections from this
book, write to Permissions, Houghton Mifflin Harcourt Publishing
Company, 215 Park Avenue South, New York, New York 10003.

www.hmhco.com

The text of this book is set in Cheltenham.
The display type was hand-lettered.
The illustrations were created digitally.

The Library of Congress Cataloging-in-Publication Data
Jahn-Clough, Lisa.
Petal and Poppy and the mystery valentine / by Lisa Clough
and Ed Briant.
p. cm. — (Green light readers. Level 3)
Summary: On Valentine's Day morning, Petal the elephant wakes up
to find chocolates and Poppy the rhinocerous finds flowers, but they
forgot to get gifts for each other, so who is their mystery Valentine?
ISBN 978-0-544-55549-5 paperback
ISBN 978-0-544-55550-1 paper over board
[1. Valentines Day—Fiction. 2. Best friends—Fiction. 3. Friendship—
Fiction. 4. Elephants—Fiction. 5. Rhinoceroses—Fiction.] I. Briant,
Ed, illustrator. II. Title.
PZ7.J153536Pfk 2015
[E]—dc23
2014037904

Manufactured in China
SCP 10 9 8 7 6 5 4 3 2 1

4500554164

7

11

12

13

15

23

25